DARK DOMINATION

Bought by the Billionaire Book One

EVERLY STONE

DARK DOMINATION

Bought by the Billionaire
Book One

By Everly Stone

ABOUT THE BOOK

Marine turned billionaire arms dealer Jackson Hawke has one goal—to have the woman who ruined his life at his mercy. He'll see her on her knees, even if he has to pay for the privilege.

Six years ago, Hannah buried her twin sister. Now, with her family in jeopardy, Hannah must sell herself to a wealthy stranger in order to save their home.

She expects to be scarred by the experience. She doesn't expect to pay penance for her sister's sins or to meet a man who brings her body savagely to life.

Now Hannah must choose—confess to Jackson that she's not the twin he's looking for and forfeit the money she needs to survive, or submit to a man whose dark domination may be the end of them both.

* *Dark Domination is the 1st in the Bought by the Billionaire serial romance series. It ends in a cliffhanger.* *

This book was previously published as Dark Domination by L. Valente. Only the author name has changed.

Dedicated to all my partners in crime.

"Keep the door locked, Hannah, and don't go outside." Her sister, Harley, dug her fingers into the soft flesh of Hannah's upper arms, the arms she could never keep as toned as her twin's, no matter how often she hit the gym. "No one can know you're here. Do you understand me? No one."

"I get it," Hannah said for the third time.

"Even if the hall is full of starving orphans," Harley insisted, her blue eyes hard and focused. "Even if there's a nun out there with her pants on fire, you keep the door closed and your mouth shut. Get me?"

"But nuns don't wear pants." Hannah winked, trying to ease the tension that had festered in the air since she'd surprised Harley at work this afternoon.

But her sister's perfectly sculpted brows only drew closer together. "I'm serious, Moo. You know I love you, but if you screw this up for me, I'm going to lose it."

"Screw what up?" Hannah asked, dread whispering through her chest.

Harley's schemes were never good news.

Her twin's flair for the dramatic had taken a dark, twisted turn that summer ten years ago when their family had fractured down the middle. Afterward, their mother had been the one most obviously damaged, but something in Harley had been broken, too.

Since then, her sister never seemed to know when she'd gone too far, or care if people were caught in the crossfire.

"What's going on?" Hannah pressed. "Is this why you've been pushing me away all summer?"

"I haven't been pushing you away," Harley lied, not even bothering to do it convincingly. When Harley was in top form, she could make you believe that the sky was green and the grass was blue.

But she didn't bother turning on the charm for family.

She saved that for the art dealers who

purchased her sculptures, the wealthy lovers she played against each other like pieces in increasingly heartbreaking games of chess, and the unlucky victims slated to pay for wronging her.

It didn't matter if the sin was real or imagined or if Harley realized halfway through crafting her blueprint for revenge that the punishment she'd conceived for her target didn't fit the crime. She never shifted direction or altered course.

Hannah was the second guesser, the person who could always see both sides of a story.

Harley was simply...inexorable.

Sometimes, it made Hannah wonder if she had absorbed her twin's share of empathy in the womb.

Sometimes it simply scared the hell out of her.

"Don't go." Hannah mirrored her sister's stance, gripping Harley's arms, but her touch remained gentle. It was her blessing and her curse, her inability to be as tough and pitiless as her father wanted his daughters to be. "Stay with me. Let's make popcorn and watch *Pretty Woman* and pretend it's the end of another perfect summer. Like when we were kids."

"It is the end of a perfect summer."

Harley's smile was sharp to the touch. "The most perfect summer ever."

She leaned in, pressing an impulsive kiss to Hannah's cheek. "I love you, Moo. And I'm never going to let anyone get away with hurting you or Mom again. Okay? Just stay inside, quiet as a mouse, and everything will be fine."

Hannah's stomach clenched. "Harley, please, I've got a bad feeling."

"You've always got a bad feeling, worry wart." She pulled away with a laugh, reaching for the black handbag on the polished table by the apartment's front door.

The apartment Harley had chosen for her summer on the Virginia shore was uncharacteristically modest, but her purse still cost a few thousand dollars. When Hannah had left for college at Duke, she had adjusted her wardrobe to fit in with the other undergraduate students in her psychology program, gratefully abandoning thousand dollar dresses for blue jeans and tee shirts.

But Harley's taste had only grown more extravagant.

Her twin was making a killing in the art world, had sweet-talked their father into granting her access to her trust fund two years early, and was always getting gifts from her endlessly shifting assortment of suitors. She was never short on money, which was another reason the modest apartment, the summer job serving drinks at a restaurant by the beach, and the beat up VW Bug Hannah had seen parked in her sister's space in the parking lot below made no sense.

Add in the tip envelope with "Harley Garrett" printed on the outside that Harley had tucked into her purse before hustling Hannah out of the bar this afternoon, and there was no doubt that Harley was up to something.

Why else would she be using a fake last name?

But Hannah knew from experience her twin wouldn't share a word about her latest scheme until it was a fait accompli.

Her sister was as superstitious as she was fearless. She wouldn't risk jinxing a plan by whispering a word about her hoped for outcome until the deed was done and the bodies were buried.

"There's leftover rice and Thai curry in the fridge," Harley said, checking her makeup in the mirror by the door, brushing away an invisible lipstick smear at the corner of her full mouth. "Feel free to have that or any of the stuff in the freezer, but don't order anything to be delivered. Once I leave, this door doesn't open until I get home tomorrow morning, not even for the pizza guy."

"I get it," Hannah said, irritation creeping in to singe the edges of her dread. "But we're going to talk when you get back. A real talk."

She'd driven six hours to spend the weekend with her sister and she wasn't going to spend her last few days of freedom before graduate school locked up in Harley's apartment, hiding from the world.

"And we're going to the beach," she added, glancing down at her pale, spent-the-summer-in-the-library arms. "I need some sun."

Harley's gaze shifted, meeting Hannah's in the glass before flicking back to her own reflection.

The eye contact only lasted a moment, but it was long enough for Hannah to be certain the next words out of Harley's mouth were going to be a lie.

"Okay. We'll go to the beach and talk. I promise." She turned, pulling Hannah in for a quick hug. "Never ever, Moo."

"Never ever," Hannah mumbled into her sister's silky brown hair before Harley slipped out the door. She couldn't help repeating the familiar phrase, no matter how frustrated she was with her twin.

Never ever was what they had said to each other since they were little girls.

It meant more than I love you.

It meant I never ever want to be apart, I never ever want to wake up to a day without you in it, I never ever want to be as close to anyone in the world as I am to you, my sister, my best friend, my other half.

But they hadn't been that close in years and lately, when Hannah thought of her sister, it was with an ache in her chest and a hollow feeling in her gut. She knew from her psychology classes that twins often had a slower, more difficult individuation process than normal siblings.

It was just harder for "we" to become "me and you" when you've spent your entire life as one half of a matched set.

But what was happening between her and Harley was about more than growing up. They were growing apart, becoming such different people that she could look down the road and see incredible pain in their future.

There would come a day when she wouldn't be able to forgive Harley for something she'd done.

A day when her sister would go too far and become someone she couldn't trust, maybe even someone she was ashamed of. Hannah had a big heart and a forgiving spirit, but even she had hard limits, lines in the sand that, once crossed, could never be uncrossed.

Later, after a supper of leftovers and a few mindless hours passed in front of the television, Hannah lay in her sister's bed, staring at the ceiling in the dark, thinking about those lines.

She didn't want to believe Harley would hurt innocent people, but as the years passed, her twin reminded her more of their any-means-to-an-end father than their sweet Aunt Sybil—the woman they'd both sworn they wanted to take after when they were girls.

They'd been eleven years old the first time they'd gone to stay with Sybil for the summer, desperate for a woman to look up to, a woman who wasn't broken and sad like their mother or cold and efficient like Nanny Hammond or the night nurses who had sat watch outside their bedroom since they were infants.

Sybil struggled with severe arthritis and other health problems, but she was always upbeat, excited to greet the day, and eager to spread light around her corner of the world. She exuded a quiet strength and was unfail-ingly kind.

If there was one thing Hannah never wanted to fail at, it was kindness.

But when did kindness become weakness?

More importantly, when did her love for and support of her sister make her an accomplice, culpable for the suffering of the people caught in Harley's warpath?

She didn't know, but she knew she and Harley were going to have a real talk tomorrow morning.

It was time for Hannah to make it clear that while her love was unconditional, her friendship and support were not.

If Harley couldn't assure her that she was keeping her hands clean, then the next time her sister called in the middle of the night, needing someone to talk her down from her latest anxiety attack or assure her that everything was going to be okay, Hannah wouldn't pick up the phone.

Sometimes, anxiety isn't meant to be banished by a gentle voice in the darkness.

Sometimes, anxiety is the soul's way of telling the body that there are dangerous choices being made, choices that could lead to pain, suffering, and destruction of the most beautiful things in your life.

* * *

*H*annah drifted off to sleep battling her own anxious thoughts and didn't expect to sleep well.

Even after four years of living in single dorms and tiny rooms in apartments she shared with friends, she still had trouble drifting off without her sister's body close to hers.

They'd slept in the same bed from the time they were born until the autumn Hannah left for college and Harley headed to New York City to set the art world on fire.

Hannah's high school boyfriend had thought the single queen bed in their shared room was strange and Harley's boys of the moment had usually thought it was sexy—no doubt imagining what it would be like to be sandwiched in between the Mason twins while they did something more than sleep.

But Harley and Hannah hadn't cared what anyone else had thought.

They simply rested more peacefully when they were close enough to feel each other's body heat, to hear the soothing sound of another heartbeat, another indrawn breath, another exhalation through softly parted lips.

Maybe it was the familiar smell of her sister's almond lotion lingering in the air that soothed Hannah into a deep sleep, or maybe it was the gentle patter of the rain on the roof that began to fall around nine thirty.

Whatever it was, Hannah was far past the REM phase, drifting in the slow, sticky waves of delta rest when she was suddenly wrenched awake by the feeling of a heavy body settling on top of her in the darkness and a huge hand covering her mouth.

CHAPTER TWO

Hannah

Hannah's eyes flew open and her lips parted in a scream, but the enormous man straddling her pressed his hand tighter to her lips, muffling the sound.

She jerked her arms downward, ready to fight him off, only to discover that her wrists were tied to the headboard. Terror rushed through her and her pulse sped, setting her heart to slamming against her ribs as she tugged harder on her bonds.

But the rope biting into her wrists assured her she wouldn't be able to fight her way free.

She was bound tight, powerless to protect herself from whatever this man intended to do to her.

"Relax, princess. It's just me." The man leaned down, the water dripping from the end of his nose, landing on Hannah's cheek, making her flinch. "I came in through the window. I thought I'd make that fantasy you were telling me about a reality."

Hannah swallowed, her thundering heartbeat slowing a bit as she understood what was happening.

She wasn't being attacked by an intruder.

This man must be Harley's guy of the moment, and he *clearly* thought he was straddling her sister.

Once she cleared up the misunderstanding, he'd untie her and she could show him to the door. They'd both be embarrassed, no doubt, but she wasn't about to be raped or murdered.

The realization made her whip-tight muscles sag with relief, an action she realized too late that the man took as an invitation to continue living out Harley's bondage fantasy.

"I've been dying to touch you all day," he said, his dry palm moving from her mouth to her breast, teasing her nipple through her thin tee shirt, drawing a gasp from her throat.

She expected his touch to feel foreign and unwelcome, but his fingers were gentle, teasing her with a sweetness that made her arch into his warm hand. Electricity shot from her breast to coil between her legs, the sensation intensified by the feel of the rope digging into her wrists as her biceps tightened reflexively in response to the stranger's confident touch.

"God, the sounds you make drive me crazy," the man said, pinching her nipple tight enough to make her gasp again.

"No, please, I'm not—" Hannah's words ended in a moan as he pushed her shirt up and bent lower, tugging her nipple into the warm, wet heat of his mouth.

His tongue flicked and teased, flooding her body with pleasure and longing so intense she was panting by the time he transferred his mouth to her other breast, sucking and nibbling at the aroused skin as his big hand slipped down the front of her panties, finding where she was already wet.

Wet, from her *sister's boyfriend's* mouth on her breasts.

And now his fingers were sliding into where she ached, making her shudder.

If she didn't stop this soon, it would be too late.

There would be no avoiding tragedy, there would be only shame and the nightmare of confessing to her sister and this innocent man that she'd done something unforgivable.

"Stop, I'm not Harley." She tensed her

thighs only to relax them a second later when she realized her locked muscles were trapping his fingers inside her embarrassingly slick sex.

"No, you're not," he said, driving his fingers in and out of her as he trapped her nipple between his teeth and bit down, making her cry out in pain before he soothed away the hurt with his tongue.

"You're my little slut," he continued in his deep, sexy rumble of a voice, his fingers still busy between her legs, making the tension coiling low in her body fist even tighter. "And I'm going to fuck you until you scream."

"No, please," Hannah said, excitement and fear dumping into her bloodstream simultaneously, making her feel like she was being deliciously, torturously torn in two. "I'm not Harley, I'm—"

This time, he silenced her with a kiss, his tongue pushing between her lips, demanding entrance to her mouth.

He tasted of something smoky, hard cider, and the ocean on a day when it isn't safe to go into the water. His kiss was dangerous, wild, and unlike anything Hannah had experienced before.

He didn't tease or test her; he fucked her mouth with his tongue, the thick muscle mimicking the movements of his fingers between her legs, bringing her to the edge faster than she'd imagined possible.

She'd had trouble tumbling over in the past. But her former boyfriends had always been sweet men and often too-tender lovers.

This man might be sweet—she had no way of knowing what he was like outside the bedroom—but he wasn't tender. He was demanding, controlling, the type of man who didn't hesitate, didn't change course, didn't stop until the job was done.

There would be no easy escape from this bed, she knew it even before he hooked his fingers inside of her, coaxing her into an orgasm that had her bowing off the bed, screaming into the hot, hungry mouth still devouring her own.

Her body clenched down, liquid heat gushing out to dampen her thighs as pleasure rocketed through her core and his tongue continued to fuck her mouth, building her need again even as her pussy still throbbed and clutched at his thick fingers.

By the time he grabbed her behind the knees, forcing her legs up and out—until her knees were in her armpits and she was bared to him, from her ass to her dripping sex— she was beyond words, beyond identity, beyond awareness of anything but the blunt head of his engorged cock hot at her entrance.

Fear flashed through her for a moment—she was on the pill, but she'd never had sex without a condom before—but then he was gliding into her, shoving through her swollen flesh, stretching her so wide she wasn't sure she'd ever be the same again.

She moaned, pain and pleasure warring within her as he claimed her in one long, slow stroke.

He was enormous and so thick her body fought to eject him, to banish the burning sensation he caused between her legs. But he kept coming. And coming and coming, until she swore she could feel him in her belly, in her lungs.

He was everywhere, his hot thickness filling her up until there was no room for anything but him.

She tried to breathe deeper, to center herself, to hold on to that sacred, hidden kernel of her soul no man had ever touched, but she couldn't find it.

There was only him, his heat, his rain and campfire smell, and his need, spearing her in two, insisting she take everything he had to give.

"Look at me," he said, holding still inside

her, his voice demanding she obey. "Look at me."

She lifted her eyes to his, a ragged sob escaping from her strained throat.

At this angle, the light from the bathroom hit his face and she was granted her first good look at him, this stranger who was buried inside her, and it all but stopped her heart.

He was beautiful—strong, rugged features softened by full lips and dark eyes that burned with passion and intelligence.

He was as stunning as all of Harley's men, but there was more to him than a handsome face or a gorgeous body. There was something in his eyes, something that made her want to know him, to please him.

"I know what you want," he said. "But I can't go there until you tell me that you're mine." He paused, looking so deep into her she couldn't believe he didn't see that she was an imposter.

But in the long, breathless moment that their eyes held and all of Hannah's secrets and fears seeped into the air between them, his gaze only gentled.

"Because you are mine," he said softly, his voice as tender as his cock was merciless. "Your pleasure belongs to me, your pain belongs to me. I want it all, Harley. All of you.

Don't fight me anymore. Give it to me. Give it all to me."

Hannah's breath rushed out through her parted lips, but she didn't know what to say, how to tell him she was a liar when this moment felt so real, so right.

"You can trust me." He flexed his buttocks, forcing his cock impossibly deeper, making her groan in pleasure.

In pain.

Pleasure-pain.

They were one and the same with this man and she wanted nothing more than to give him what he wanted, whatever he wanted so long as he would never stop hurting her, healing her, possessing her in a way she'd never realized she wanted to be possessed until this stranger had claimed her for his own.

But she wasn't his and he wasn't hers.

He belonged to her sister and this was so wrong that "wrong" wasn't a big enough word to describe it—this betrayal, this sacrilege, this terrible, terrible thing she'd allowed to happen.

She should have fought harder, screamed the truth until he understood she wasn't playing games.

Now it was too late, and she hated herself for it.

"Please," she said, tears filling her eyes. "Forgive me."

"For what, princess?" His warm palm cupped her cheek with a sweetness that threatened to break her heart all over again.

"I can't..." She swallowed, searching for the strength to tell him the truth, but she couldn't, not when she was exposed, so vulnerable, and so intimately connected to this man that she couldn't tell where he ended and she began. "I can't tell you. Not now."

"Now is the time to tell me anything," he said, leaning down, his lips hovering above hers as he shifted his hips, pulling out until she was acutely aware of all the places that ached in his absence before pushing back into her again, summoning another hungry sound from her throat. "Everything. I'm ready for your secrets."

"No, you're not," she whispered, shuddering as he began to roll his hips, nudging her clit with his pubic bone again and again, building the need swelling inside of her.

"I'm not a fool." He captured her nipple between his fingers, tugging it in time to the undulating rhythm of his hips. "I know you've been hiding things from me. It doesn't matter.

What matters is right now. Tell me you're mine and we'll figure the rest out together."

"Stop, please," she said, teeth digging into her bottom lip as she strained against her bonds, but the rough rope against her skin only made her hotter, wetter. "I can't think. I can't—"

"Don't think," he said, his grip tightening on her nipple as he rode her harder, until she was quivering beneath him, so close to the edge she knew she could go at any moment. "Feel. Feel how real this is and tell me you're mine. Tell me and I'll do all those things you've been dreaming about."

He shifted his head, whispering into her ear, his breath hot on her skin as he fucked her with long, languid strokes that completely unraveled her mind. "I'll spank you and mark you and fuck you so hard you won't be able to sit down for days without thinking about how I used you." He pressed a kiss to her throat, where her pulse raced. "Isn't that what you want?"

Hannah nodded breathlessly.

She had never even imagined things like that, but suddenly, lying beneath this man, she wanted all the wicked things he'd promised and more.

She wanted to be turned over his knee and

punished for the lies she'd told.

She wanted him to hurt her for letting him believe she was someone she wasn't, and then she wanted him to take the pain away with his beautiful mouth.

That exquisite mouth that made her shudder now as his teeth dragged lightly over the skin at her throat.

"Then say it," he said. "Give yourself to me. Tell me you're mine."

"I'm yours," Hannah said, the words out of her mouth before she could stop them. "I'm yours. Forever. Yours."

"Fuck yes, princess," he moaned, thrusting faster, deeper, demanding her pleasure. "Come for me. Come on my cock. Let me feel you."

Hannah's head fell back as she came with a sound that wasn't cute or ladylike.

It was wild and base, a cry of animal satisfaction that ripped from her throat as her pussy clutched at her stranger's pistoning cock, demanding his orgasm with the same assurance that he'd ordered her own.

He came crying out her sister's name, his thickness jerking hard inside of her, the feel of his scalding heat soaking her insides sending her soaring a third time.

Lights danced behind her tightly closed eyes, and somewhere deep inside of her,

things she needed to live lost purchase and
floated away from their moorings.

She was adrift, helpless to defend herself,
totally at the mercy of this man who gently
untied her arms and kissed the red welts on
her wrists.

And she didn't even know his name.

CHAPTER THREE

Hannah

Hours later, after he'd had her again—this time with his hand fisted in her hair while he took her from behind, his rough use making her feel safer than every considerate kiss from every ex-boyfriend she'd ever had—that's all she could think about.

She didn't know the name of the man who kissed her like she was his world before climbing back out the window he'd crept through hours before.

And she wasn't going to find out until tomorrow, when she would be forced to come clean to her sister and confess the nightmarish thing she'd done.

Harley might actually forgive her—she didn't tend to get too attached to her lovers, especially the summer boys she used to entertain her between epic trips abroad—but the stranger would hate her.

He was in love with her sister.

He thought he'd been making love to Harley, not a complete stranger.

As Hannah lay in the dark, in sheets that still smelled of sex and sweat, she was forced to admit that she was a terrible person. She wasn't the good twin, after all.

She was weak and selfish and obviously unfit to become a psychiatrist and counsel troubled kids, not when she was so messed up in the head that she'd slept with her sister's boyfriend.

The first time, he hadn't given her time to protest, but she could have stopped things before they came together again, before he held her on his chest and promised she would always be under his protection, or before she whispered "I love you, too" as he eased out onto the tree limb beneath the second story window.

Liar.

She was such a miserable liar.

She didn't know if Harley loved the man, but Hannah barely knew him. It was impossible to love a man you had just met and barely spoken to aside from some scalding hot pillow talk.

She knew that, but as she got up to put the sheets on to wash and start a pot of coffee—sleep was going to be impossible, might as well help the insomnia along—she couldn't help wishing that she didn't have to tell her stranger the truth.

A selfish, wicked part of her secretly hoped that Harley would never come back to her summer apartment, that she would hop the next flight to Paris and disappear the way she sometimes did, usually right when Hannah needed her the most.

And then Hannah could meet the man again, learn his name, and start figuring out what it would take to make him hers.

* * *

In the years to come, she would think of that selfish, wicked wish again and again, wondering if wishes like that had a power others didn't.

Wondering if her greedy longing was the reason her sister had been murdered and Hannah would never see her best friend's face again.

Even when her Aunt Sybil spirited her

away from Harley's very private, very secret wake, insisting it was past time she learned about the darkness that haunted their family, Hannah couldn't bring herself to blame fate or her father's enemies for her sister's death.

She would never forget that one wonderful, terrible night, or that she had wished that Harley would disappear and that hours later she had.

Forever.

CHAPTER FOUR

Hannah

Six years later

Freedom doesn't come for free.

Neither does forgiveness.

Every step Hannah had taken from the moment she'd learned Harley was dead, to the morning she awoke to find Aunt Sybil crying on the back steps of their storm-battered bed and breakfast, had been taken with one goal in mind: Absolution.

She wanted more than survival.

She wanted release.

She wanted to shed her skin and leave the sins of her former life far behind her.

But the past has long arms and sharp claws that dig in deep and hold on tight. The past was a monkey on her back. A monkey with an ugly sense of humor she swore she could hear cackling at her attempts to escape the Mason family curse.

In the past six years, The Mahana Guesthouse had been damaged by gale force winds, lost three cottages in an electrical fire, suffered through two Dengue fever outbreaks that scared the tourists away for months, and nearly been reclaimed by the sea when Hurricane Isra swept through last week.

The morning after the storm, the Laurents, their only neighbors close enough to reach the guesthouse on foot, had come to check on Sybil and Hannah. The sweet older couple had wept with relief when they found the women huddled in the cottage farthest from the beach—the only structure not falling in on itself—soaked to the skin but safe. The Laurents had taken them to their home, fed them fresh French bread and guava fruit salad, and spent the rest of the day telling them how lucky they were to be alive.

But life was fragile, especially when you were a Mason.

Their savings had finally run out after the last Dengue fever outbreak. Now, if Sybil and Hannah couldn't find the money to repair the main house and guest cottages, their income would disappear, and their lives not long after.

They could never return to the states or reach out to their family for help. They were dead to the world they'd known before. This was their safe place, their one chance to carve out an existence far from the people determined to destroy them.

But if Hannah didn't figure something out soon, their safe haven would be a thing of the past.

She had to pull it together, get creative, and whip up a miracle with nothing but her hands, a dash of hope, and an abundance of determination.

But first, she had to make sure her aunt didn't hurl herself into the sea in despair.

"I come bearing gifts." She held the steaming cup of coffee beneath Sybil's nose, grateful when her aunt reached up to take the mug instead of staring zombie-like at the horizon the way she had for most of the week since the storm.

"I'm going to figure out a way to get the money today," Hannah added, curling her hands around her own warm mug. "I promise."

She had promised the same thing yesterday, but so far she'd come up with nothing.

Their tiny Tahitian island was a paradise, true, but it was also a place where jobs were few and hard to come by. And even if Hannah could manage to land a job as a maid or bartender at the luxury resort on the south shore, she wouldn't be able to cover basic expenses, let alone the cost of repairs, and the burden of raising the money sat firmly on her shoulders.

Sybil could sell her homemade banana bread and other baked goods, but she couldn't hold down a job.

Her aunt's arthritis made for days where she could barely get out of bed, let alone work ten hours stripping beds and cleaning toilets.

"I had a dream last night." Aunt Sybil swept the tears from her tanned cheeks with a trembling hand.

"Not a good dream, I'm guessing." Hannah sat down beside her on the steps leading down to the beach.

"No, it was," Sybil said, her gaze trained on the waves lapping at the sugar-white shore. "Aaron, Ezra, and Matthew were alive. We were at the old house eating dinner on the lawn the way we used to in the summers when we were young. But in the dream, we were all grown up and there were children and grand-children everywhere." She smiled. "Dozens of dirty bare feet and popsicle sticky hands. It was lovely."

Hannah sighed, knowing the sound would be masked by the wind rustling the palm leaves.

They hadn't lost all the trees. Or the pool. That, at least, was lucky.

She was determined to stay positive.

She couldn't think about all the things that had been lost.

She couldn't think about the dead uncles she'd never met or that Harley might still be alive if Sybil had embraced her conspiracy theorist side sooner.

Before Harley's car crash and the series of "accidents" that had picked off their first cousins one by one, Hannah wouldn't have believed that there was a contract killer out there somewhere determined to kill off their entire family.

She would have thought her aunt was paranoid at best, delusional at worst. She never would have dropped out of grad school and fled the country without saying a word to anyone—even her mother and father—before the day she was forced to pick out her twin sister's coffin.

No, there was nothing to be gained from the "what could have been" game and dreams like her aunt's only made the waking world seem like more of a nightmare.

"I'm going to head into town to talk to Hiro this morning," Hannah said. "He said he might have some good news for me from his friends on Moorea. Do you need anything from the store while I'm there? Flour? Sugar?"

Sybil frowned but didn't turn her gaze away from the shore. "What kind of good news? You told him we weren't selling, right?"

"I did." Hanna ran her fingers idly back and forth across the wood beneath her.

The planks still smelled of fresh stain and were one of the few parts of the guesthouse she'd been able to rebuild herself.

She was handy, but she wasn't a trained carpenter or a roofer or a plumber or any of the other endless skilled laborers they'd need to hire to make sure their tiny resort was ready to receive guests.

Still, she understood why her aunt didn't want to sell.

After the hurricane, property values were in the gutter. They'd never get what the resort was worth and it was dangerous for them to conduct any business with a paper trail.

Both she and Sybil had fake passports with assumed names, but anything that made people pay attention was a bad idea.

That's why they had kept to the tradition Hannah's father had started long ago and never posted pictures of themselves on the Internet. They didn't have host photos on their website, refused to be photographed with their guests, and conducted all of their transactions in cash.

Cash that was growing perilously low.

"I'm not sure what he had in mind, but he seemed hopeful," Hannah said, forcing an upbeat note into her voice. "And if anyone can be trusted to help us wiggle out of this, it's Hiro. You know how much he wants you to stay on the island."

Sybil grunted, but Hannah could tell her aunt was fighting a smile. "You'd think after a year of trying he'd get the message that nothing's going to happen between us. He's half my age, for goodness' sake."

"He's only ten years younger," Hannah corrected, nudging her aunt's knee gently with her own. "And he might get the idea if you'd stop flirting with him like a shameless hussy."

Her aunt's answering laughter was one of the sweetest sounds Hannah had heard in days.

"Oh my goodness," Sybil said, still giggling. "I didn't think anyone had noticed."

"Kind of hard to miss," Hannah said, grinning. "I think it's adorable and I bet you and Hiro would have a lot of fun together. And how many people can say they've dated a pearl farmer?"

Sybil's smile faded as she tucked her gray-streaked blond curls behind her ears.

She really did look so much younger than fifty-five, with only lightly wrinkled skin and bright blue eyes that danced when she was happy. She swore that her commitment to looking on the bright side had kept her young, which only made it harder to see her succumbing to despair and losing faith that everything would work out okay in the end.

"Maybe I'll think about it," her aunt finally said in a soft voice. "If we're still here come the new year."

"But it's only November. You know you don't have to wait until New Year's Eve to try something new, right?" Hannah pressed. "Why don't you let me invite Hiro to come have dinner on the beach with us tonight? It's supposed to be a beautiful evening, and I'll be there to chaperone."

"Oh no," Sybil said shaking her head. "I don't even have a proper kitchen to cook in. I can't feed a guest anything I've whipped up on the hot plate."

"Give him a few beers first and I doubt he'll notice he's eating grilled cheese," Hannah said, finishing her last sip of coffee. "Besides, it's the company he's after, not the gourmet experience."

Sybil's head shaking grew more agitated. "No, Hannah. I'm not ready. Maybe someday, but not now. Not until we know you're safe."

Hannah's spirits fell and she suddenly wished she hadn't pushed.

She knew her aunt wasn't comfortable with change and even less comfortable with men. Besides, Hannah wasn't in any position to preach about embracing opportunities for romance.

She had only dated two men since the move and both relationships had lasted only a few months before fizzling away.

She told herself it was the need for anonymity and secrecy that made it hard to forge a connection. She refused to admit how often she thought about the night she'd promised herself to a stranger.

Or how often she woke up from erotic dreams featuring *his* hands on her body and his lips on her skin.

Her mystery lover, the one who had ruined her for other men.

But she wasn't going to think about him either.

Positive thoughts were the order of the day.

* * *

*S*he managed to keep her head up and her optimistic attitude firmly in place until her meeting with an anxious, embarrassed Hiro, who told her what he'd learned from his connections on Moorea.

There was a way for Hannah and Sybil to save the resort: a billionaire who was willing to give them the money they would need to rebuild.

But what he wanted in exchange was something Hannah had never imagined putting up for sale.

"I don't know if I can do that," she said, glancing over her shoulder, hoping no one else at the open air café had heard Hiro's proposal or her response.

She wouldn't even be considering what the pearl farmer had suggested if she weren't backed so far into a corner she was starting to fear she'd never get out.

When she was certain none of the other patrons of the café were listening, she turned back to Hiro and whispered, "What kind of man is he? Do you know him? Would I be safe?"

"Yes, he's a good man. A very good man. And very rich." Hiro's dark eyes tightened with concern. "But it is too much, yeah? You are a good girl." He ran a tanned hand through his lightly graying hair. "Your aunt would be so angry with me if she knew I'd even mentioned this kind of arrangement."

Hannah shook her head as she picked nervously at an empty sugar packet. "Sybil could never know. If I do this, if I become..." She swallowed hard, unable to speak the words "erotic companion" aloud. "I'd have to make up another excuse for leaving the island. I couldn't let her find out. It would kill her."

And it might kill you.

You trust Hiro, but do you trust his assessment of a stranger's character enough to risk your life on it?

She wasn't sure, but after they had finished their tea and she'd walked down the crowded village street to the grocery store and checked her and Sybil's bank balance at the ATM, she knew she had no choice but to accept the terrifying offer.

They were almost broke.

There was no other way to pay for Sybil's medicines, let alone get their business up and running again.

And it would only be for a month. She could do anything for a month.

Pushing away throat-tightening images of a greasy man with a hairy back ordering her to spread her legs, Hannah pulled out her cell and dialed Hiro's number.

"I'll do it," she said when the farmer answered. "I'll pick up the directions on my way out of town."

It was time, the moment Jackson Hawke had been working toward for six long years.

He was finally going to have his revenge on the woman who had taken everything that mattered away from him and set his life on fire.

The woman whose death he'd mourned even as the wounds she'd left on his heart teemed with hatred, unlike anything he'd ever known.

During his ten years in the Marines, Jackson had been deployed to some of the most violent war zones in the world and seen men commit acts so heinous they deserved no mercy, no trial, no second chance. He'd come face to face with human monsters, but Harley Garrett was the worst of them all.

She was pure poison, venom wrapped in an irresistibly beautiful shell. She was a nightmare come to life, but he'd cried when he'd learned she'd been killed in the car wreck that had claimed the life of his best friend. Still, he'd ached to hold her, even after learning she and Clay had been on their way to Niagara Falls to get married when their car was forced off a dangerous mountain road.

It wasn't until Jackson was locked in a cage, disowned by his family and reviled by his friends, that he'd stopped grieving and started hating with a purity that had transformed hatred into a religion. Hate became his center, his mantra, and the reason he'd been able to rise from the ashes of his former life to become something stronger and better than he'd been before.

He no longer had an honor code, morals, or ethics standing in the way of taking what he wanted. Now, he had hate and the single-minded focus it lent all its devotees.

Without that focus, he wouldn't have kept digging into the details of Harley's death until he discovered that Harley Garrett had been born out of the ether that summer six years ago. He wouldn't have learned that there wasn't a single photograph of the woman on the web or a record of her body being buried anywhere in the United States. He wouldn't have made contact with the kind of men who made a living finding people who didn't want to be found or kept paying them to search for Harley for years after a less vitriol-filled man would have given up hope of finding the monster who had gotten away.

And without hate, he never would have learned that Harley was living the sweet life on a tiny island in Tahiti or had the patience to wait until she was vulnerable and powerless to fight him to take his revenge.

Initially, he'd planned to buy her property for a song and drag out closing negotiations until she and her aging aunt were so desperate to survive that Harley would have no choice but to agree to his demands.

But this...

This was so much better.

His cock thickened at the thought of all the things he was going to do to Harley's tight little body once she belonged to him. He hated her, but he still wanted to fuck her, to get his cock in her lying mouth, into her slick cunt, into the pretty pink asshole she'd denied him access to years ago, back when he'd cared what she wanted. He was going to have her every filthy way he'd imagined and make all the lies she'd told come true, until she regretted ever hearing the name Jackson Hawke, let alone ruining his life.

Once upon a time, his dark desires would have troubled him. But now he didn't care if it was twisted to want his enemy on her knees in front of him choking on his cock.

He didn't care about anything except seeing that bitch get what she deserved.

"She's on her way up, sir." His pilot and right-hand man, Adam, stepped into the artificially cool hotel room, his tanned face shiny from the late afternoon heat. "Is there anything else you need before I head down to the field?"

Jackson shook his head. "No. Just be ready for takeoff when we show up. If all goes well, we'll be there before sunset."

Adam nodded and stepped out of the room without another word. It was one of the things that made the man invaluable to him. Whether they were smuggling guns to drug lords in South America, selling secrets to rebels in war-torn countries, or arranging to buy a woman for a million dollars and change, Adam didn't put his oar in. He did as he was told, got the job done, and kept his mouth shut.

It made for boring company, but Jackson wasn't worried about it being just the three of them and a small number of carefully selected support staff on a private island for a month.

He expected Harley would keep him more than entertained.

Jackson turned to the computer monitor on the desk in front of him, waiting for his prey to appear, wondering if she'd follow the directions she'd been given like a good girl. The Harley he'd known had chosen defiance over obedience at every opportunity, but the woman he'd known had been a cipher, a lie from beginning to end.

Soon he would get to know the real Harley and maybe even learn why she'd made it her mission on earth to destroy him.

Not that he cared anymore.

He couldn't care less if his name was cleared—he'd done his share to tarnish his formerly pristine reputation in the past few years—but he would still make her return to Virginia with him to meet his father. He needed to see the look on Ian Hawke's face when he learned that a lying whore had tricked him into disowning his son. That alone would be worth more than a million dollars.

As if summoned by his thoughts of lying whores, the door opened in the room on his screen and a woman in a simple, sleeveless black sundress stepped inside.

CHAPTER SIX

Jackson

The moment her tensed, frightened features turned to face the camera set up beside the bed, he knew it was Harley.

Still, something in his gut pinged, insisting this wasn't the woman he'd been hunting for.

But for once, Jackson ignored the gut instinct that had kept him alive and out of prison during the years he'd enthusiastically embraced a life of crime.

It was no wonder his gut was confused.

Harley had changed significantly in the past six years.

Her once dark brown hair had turned auburn in the island sun and freckles covered her tanned face, making her eyes look even more strikingly blue than they had before.

But it was her body that had changed the most.

Gone were the relatively boyish figure and stick legs she'd complained about when they used to go walking on the beach. In their place were curves for miles and miles.

She'd been beautiful before.

But now she was...a goddess.

She was exactly the kind of woman he'd always preferred, with abundant breasts that would overflow even his large hands, generous hips, and a curvy ass he couldn't wait to get turned over his knee.

As soon as they reached his island, he was going to give her that spanking she'd begged for back when they were lovers.

But this time he wouldn't stop before pleasure-pain turned to suffering.

He would keep reddening her ass until her flesh glowed and she squirmed on his lap, begging him to release her. But he wouldn't, not until he'd bruised her sensitive skin, making sure that every time she sat down for the next week she'd be reminded that she was his property, to do with as he saw fit.

The thought was dizzying.

And so arousing that by the time Harley reached for the top of her dress with trembling hands, his cock was testing the integrity of his zipper.

Slowly, slowly, doing exactly as she'd been told, she pulled her dress down to reveal her breasts, then her tanned stomach, and finally her full hips before pushing the fabric past her thighs. It fell down to puddle around her ankles, taking Jackson's breath away.

She had obeyed the order not wear anything under the dress, as well, so the moment the black fabric dropped to the floor, she was bare to his gaze.

From her stunning breasts with the dark pink nipples to the gentle curve of her belly to the small thatch of dark hair that covered her mound, she was perfect.

Jackson's throat tightened and a wave of lust swept through him, making his skin feverishly hot.

He wanted her.

Now.

He wanted to abandon this chair, hurry down the hallway to the sunlit room where Harley stood trembling in front of that camera, and show her how much more scared she should be.

He wanted to see her face when she realized who had come to claim her and then he wanted to bend her over that mosquito-netted bed in the corner and fuck her, hard and deep, until he lost himself inside of her, marking his new pet with his cum.

Instead, he forced himself to relax, to exert control.

Revenge wasn't something to be taken fast and hot.

As the saying went, revenge was a dish best served cold.

When Harley laid eyes on him for the first time in six years, he would be cold, glacial. He would give her no power, no hope of using his emotions to manipulate him.

She would never know how deeply she'd hurt him or how much he still wanted her.

When he did eventually fuck her, it would be calm, efficient, a means to an end, a step on the path to breaking her.

He would not give her his need or his hate.

He would give her nothing but what she had given him—suffering and pain.

And so he sat completely still as he watched Harley bring her hands to her breasts, ignoring the fact that the sight of her small hands cupping her full mounds made his balls ache.

He remained frozen as she rolled her nipples between her fingers until her breath came faster and the anxiety on her face was replaced with arousal.

But when she dropped one hand between her legs and began to rub her clit in circles, clearly intending to reach orgasm the way her instructions had commanded, his control snapped.

As Harley plucked at her nipple and fingered herself, he stood, wrenching open his fly.

His swollen cock bobbed free, so hard and hot the skin felt like it would burn his palm as he took himself in hand and began to stroke his engorged length in time to the rhythm Harley had set. He jerked harder, faster, his cock swelling in his own hand as he imagined what it would be like to be in the same room as his prey.

Would he be able to smell her wet cunt, salty and sticky-sweet in the air?

Would he be able to hear the sound of her fingers gliding through her slick, swollen flesh?

See the flush that spread across her chest right before she came?

Would he have rushed in to catch her as her legs buckled and she dropped to the floor, crying out in ecstasy and fear as her orgasm brought her to her knees?

Or would he have simply stepped in and

finished with his cock level with her face, shooting his release across her pink cheeks and between her parted lips?

He groaned as he came—hard, exploding in his own hand, his cum splashing across the computer screen, covering Harley's face before leaking down to coat her breasts.

It wasn't as good as the real thing, but it was still pretty fucking amazing.

She'd followed his orders and now she would be his.

And in a few days—or a few hours, however long he was able to last—he would have her on her knees in front of him, ready to take whatever he would give her.

Jackson fetched a towel from the bathroom and cleaned up his mess, watching Harley get dressed with stiff, jerky motions that made him think she was embarrassed by what she'd just done.

Good.

Embarrassment wasn't shame, but it was moving in the right direction.

Her downcast gaze and flushed cheeks made him smile as he placed the final call to set his revenge in motion. "Hello, this is Mr. Hawke. Release the hundred thousand to the Mahana Guesthouse account."

"Right away, sir," the banker promised in heavily accented English.

Jackson could have spoken to the man in his native French—he had become fluent in both French and German during the years he studied at West Point—but he wasn't interested in making other people's lives any easier.

Jackson thanked him and hung up before texting Hiro.

It was time for his spy to make one final phone call.

The man had obviously begun to regret the part he'd played in the sale of Harley Garrett—or Hannah North as she was calling herself these days—but another deposit in the pearl farmer's account had convinced him to ignore his protective instincts and get the job done.

Moments after the text went through, the phone in Harley's room rang.

She crossed to the bedside table, bringing her closer to the camera as she answered the phone, close enough for him to see the faint tan line creeping around her neck.

When she was his, she wouldn't have tan lines. He didn't plan on allowing her the luxury of being clothed. At least, not at first. Whether she was inside the house they would share or out on the beach scanning the deserted horizon for signs of a rescue that would never come, she would do it in the nude.

"Oh, okay," she said, nodding though the man on the other end of the line obviously couldn't see her. "I'll meet the car downstairs in a few minutes. Thank you, Hiro. For everything."

The other man said something Jackson couldn't hear but that seemed to make Harley more nervous. Her voice was shaking when she spoke again. "Okay. I will. Look out for Aunt Sybil for me. I'll see you both soon."

She hung up, hesitating only a moment before picking up the phone and dialing another number. In light, lilting French she asked for the banker who had helped set up the funds transfer from Hawke's Swiss bank account to the bed and breakfast's local Tahitian one.

Clearly she didn't trust the mysterious billionaire who had offered to purchase her escort services for the month.

Hawke smiled again.

She shouldn't trust him. Everything he'd told Hiro about wanting a beautiful American girl for a month of fun, sun, and no-strings-attached consensual vanilla sex on the beach was a lie. But when it came to the money he had kept his promise to pay one tenth of the fee up front.

He knew Harley well enough to realize she would never get in his car or on his plane unless she knew she'd been paid something for her trouble.

She was a liar, but she was no fool.

She spoke again and was apparently assured that all the money ducks were in a row, because she thanked the banker, hung up the phone, and turned to go. She hesitated for a moment, but then her hands balled into fists, her chin lifted, and she started for the door with a steady stride, obviously determined to meet the man who had bought her with her head held high.

Too bad Hawke would be taking a separate car to the airport and that Harley would be blindfolded and gagged before he arrived at the airstrip.

He wasn't taking any chances that she would see his face and try to call for help while they were still surrounded by friendly islanders who might come to the rescue of a woman in need.

She wouldn't have the use of her voice

until they landed on Le Sauvage, an isolated island at the far edge of the archipelago, where no one would be able to hear her scream.

CHAPTER SEVEN

Hannah

Hannah climbed into the back of the stretch limo waiting in the shade beside the Pension La Plage on rubbery legs. By the time the silent driver wound his way through the colorful streets of Fare, down jungle roads tunneled in green, and out to the private jet waiting at the edge of the airfield, she was trembling all over and fighting the urge to dash across the airstrip and make a run for the safety of the tiny airport waiting room.

What the hell had she done?

What you had to do. You're just lucky there was a man willing to pay that kind of price for a twenty-eight-year-old woman with no experience as an escort.

An escort. It was just a kinder word for a whore. Tonight—or maybe this afternoon, depending on whether or not the man who'd bought her joined her on the private jet—she would have sex with a man for money. It was a lot of money—once he paid the remainder of her fee she would have enough to save the guesthouse and make sure she and Sybil were safe from the ravages of their own bad luck for years—but still...

Still, she felt filthy, ashamed, and dangerously foolish.

She'd been bought and paid for. She had sold herself to a complete stranger. A man who had already seen her naked and watched while she pleasured herself in front of the camera he'd set up in his hotel room. In the grand scheme of things it wasn't that kinky, she supposed, but it was kinkier than anything she'd done before, and it had made her vulnerable to this man in a way she'd never been to anyone.

He'd seen her naked, completely exposed as she'd come on her own hand, and she had never seen his face. Didn't even know his name.

You didn't know your stranger's name, either, and it didn't matter. It was still the hottest sex you've ever had.

As she climbed the steps into the private jet, Hannah swallowed hard, but the bitter taste on her tongue remained. She wasn't naïve enough to believe the billionaire who'd bought her would be a handsome young man with magic hands and a tender light in his eyes. He was almost certainly at least a decade older and probably not much to look at or he would have been able to convince a woman to come to his private island for free.

He might be hideously ugly, obese, or so ancient he'd have trouble getting aroused and she'd be forced to ignore the old-man scent of him as he labored above her, sweating and grunting.

Or maybe he was simply a twisted monster looking for a woman he could use, torture, and throw away, a woman no one would go looking for when she went missing.

Hannah half fell into the sumptuous leather seat on the far side of the plane, her trembling becoming a full-blown quake. By the time the tanned man with the close-cropped blond hair stepped out of the cockpit, she was shaking so hard her teeth were chattering.

Her eyes flew wide as her gaze connected with the man's paler, bluer one, but before she could think of what to say—or fully experience her relief at discovering that her client was a perfectly attractive middle-aged man—he crossed to stand in front of her seat.

"My employer asked that I help you tie this over your eyes." He held out a thick strip of heavy black cloth. "I've got another for your mouth."

Hannah's breath sped. "Why do I need to be blindfolded?" she asked, not wanting to think about the gagging part. The thought of not being able to speak, or even swallow her own saliva, was ridiculously terrifying, almost as scary as taking her clothes off in front of a camera, knowing a stranger was watching.

God, what had she done? What the hell had she done?

"I don't ask questions," the man said, his voice humorless and his blue eyes remaining flat. "My employer doesn't enjoy questions. He prefers efficiency."

"All...all right." Hannah's heart raced as she reached for the blindfold, figuring it was better if she was the one to tie it on. She wrapped the soft fabric across her eyes and tied it behind her head, tight enough to be sure it wouldn't accidentally fall off, but not so tight that it pressed against her closed lids.

When she was finished, she held out her hand, willing her voice not to shake as she said, "I can tie the gag, too. If that's okay."

"Just make sure it stays put," the man said.

Hannah couldn't help flinching as the man dropped the cloth into her outstretched hand. Not being able to see was already heightening her other senses, making the sensation of soft fabric brushing against her skin ricochet through her nervous system in a way it normally wouldn't.

She tied the gag as loosely as she dared, but when she was finished her tongue still felt cramped, forced to coil at the back of her throat like a snake denied the right to strike. The combination of the stressful day, having half her face covered, her eyesight stolen away, and her mouth filled with fabric combined to trigger the worst case of claustrophobia she'd experienced since she was eight years old and Harley had accidentally locked her in the crawl space next to their room.

She'd sat in the cramped portion of the attic, where she and her sister had hidden their secret treasures from their nanny, for hours, sweating and crying in the summer heat until she'd almost passed out. But she hadn't dared call out for someone to rescue her. She'd known Harley would kill her if she let any of the staff find out about their secret hideout. Harley didn't tolerate broken promises, no matter how many she broke herself.

Hannah struggled to swallow, fighting to slow her racing, panicked heartbeat. But it was an exercise in futility. Her heart was beyond her control, like the rest of her life, and the best she could hope for was that she would pass out before her owner joined her on the plane.

The thought made her throat feel even tighter and sweat bead around her hairline and above her parted lips. By the time she heard the door to the plane open a few minutes later, she was sweating profusely, panting through her flared nostrils, and so dizzy she didn't know how much longer she would remain conscious.

She whimpered and pointed frantically to the gag, praying the blond man would understand that she was having trouble breathing and grant her permission to remove it.

But instead of the first man's firm monotone, she was answered by a low grumble, "The gag stays in. You need to relax. You're breathing too fast."

Hannah tried to relax, she really did, but this man's voice wasn't one that inspired relaxation. He sounded hard, cold, and enormous. Until this moment, she hadn't realized that a voice could project size, but this man sounded ten feet tall and bulletproof. He sounded like someone capable of strangling the life out of her with one hand and mean enough to enjoy it.

As the thought passed through her head, her traitorous breath sped even faster and her chest began to shake.

"You're going to hyperventilate if you keep that up," the man grumbled again, his voice so deep she could feel it vibrating through her bones, touching her in places a voice shouldn't be able to touch. "Hannah stop. Right now."

A whimper escaped her cramped throat and her breath came so fast it felt like she was being spun in circles by one of those terrible carnival rides she'd hated when she was a child.

"Stop it," the man repeated, his voice closer and dropped to a soothing whisper. "I'm not going to hurt you on this plane, Hannah. I give you my word."

On this plane. He hadn't said he wouldn't hurt her at all, just not on the plane, and she sensed that she wasn't reading more into the remark than he'd intended. This was a man who knew what he wanted and was willing to pay a million dollars to have a woman at his mercy. He had deliberately left the door open for pain.

Hannah clutched the arms of her chair until her fingers ached, fighting to keep from ripping the gag and blindfold off and making a break for freedom. A deal was a deal. This man had paid for the pleasure of terrifying her. And if she backed out of their agreement, she had no doubt he would take the rest of his money and leave her and Sybil to starve.

She'd made her bed and now she had to lie in it.

To sleep with this man in it, even if the thought terrified her.

"We're ready for takeoff." The first man's voice sounded too far away to still be in the plane, but maybe that was because Hannah was so focused on the new voice, her owner's voice whispering in her ear again.

"Sit back. I'll put your seatbelt on."

She leaned back in the plush seat. A moment later, she felt fingers brushing her hips as the man found both halves of the seatbelt and brought them together across her waist. His touch was calm, impersonal. He touched her only as much as he needed to in order to get the seatbelt snug across her lap, but for some reason she still shivered.

There was something about this man,

something in the spicy, salty smell of him that drifted to her nose as he settled into the seat across from hers that made her skin prickle and the hair at the back of her neck stand on end. She felt more than watched; she felt hunted and suddenly didn't know what she feared more—the nameless, faceless people who had killed half her family, or the nameless, faceless man whose foot brushed every so lightly against her own as the plane rumbled down the airstrip.

It wasn't until they were lifting off that Hannah realized the two might be one and the same.

She might have just sold herself to the man who had killed her family and the past six years of hiding, deferring all her dreams, and abandoning the aunt who needed her, might have been for nothing.

CHAPTER EIGHT

Jackson

The plane was still gaining altitude when Harley started trembling again.

She was shaking so hard he would have thought she was having a seizure if he didn't know better.

But according to everything Hiro had told him, "Hannah" was in perfect health.

It was her aunt who was frail.

So either she was truly scared out of her mind…or she was faking it to elicit sympathy from the man who'd bought her.

That would be like her.

She was a master manipulator.

Until he'd met Harley, Jackson had been certain he could spot a con around a blind corner.

His mother had majored in emotional manipulation at Brown and his sociopath father had taught him early on the importance of realizing when you were being worked like a puppet on a string.

By age ten, Jackson was a master at spotting reverse psychology; by twelve, he'd perfected his poker face; and by his fourteenth birthday, he had a plan in place to escape his father's influence: a con of his own Ian hadn't seen coming until Jackson's acceptance letter to an exclusive military boarding school showed up in the afternoon mail.

But despite all his experience with the care and feeding of sociopaths, Harley had still worked him like a player piano, arranging things so perfectly he'd practically conned himself.

Like that last night, when she'd promised to belong to him forever, fucked his heart from his chest and down to the floor to lie helpless at her feet, only to run away with his best friend a few minutes after Jackson had climbed out of her bedroom window.

She had literally gone from coming on his cock to waltzing out the door with Clay moments later.

He'd done that math.

She had to have left her apartment no later

than midnight in order to be driving down that particular stretch of highway at three in the morning.

But even after years of turning over various possible scenarios, he still had no idea exactly how she'd faked her death.

That alone was enough reason not to underestimate her capacity for treachery.

He couldn't let down his guard or allow compassion to creep into his heart.

He had to be on his toes and ready to beat Harley at her own game.

And he had a good idea how to start…

He leaned in, placing a gentle hand on her knee.

She tensed and made a startled sound behind her gag.

But after a moment, she settled beneath his touch. Her muscles remained tight, but she stopped shaking and held very still, clearly waiting for him to make the next move.

With a hard smile, he reached behind her, into her thick, soft hair, and untied her gag.

He set it on the seat beside her before returning his hand to her knee, allowing his fingers to curl around the shapely muscle of her calf.

"Is that better?" he asked

She swallowed and swiped the back of one

hand across her mouth before nodding a little too fast. "Y-yes. Thank you."

She sounded so scared, so young and vulnerable.

Like a woman who had never walked a dark street at midnight, let alone become one of the evil things lurking in the shadows.

No wonder the military police had believed every word she'd said. Even without the evidence she'd doctored, her witness statement alone was fucking compelling.

She'd been so beautiful in the tapes he'd been forced to watch. So beautiful and broken that he'd understood why the people in charge of investigation couldn't help wanting to sweep in and do whatever it took to deliver justice.

But her suffering was a lie.

Like everything else about Harley.

She was a monster hiding behind a pretty face and he knew better than to let her play him so easily.

"You're welcome," he said, gentling his voice, letting her think she was getting through to him while still keeping his pitch lower than usual.

He expected her to recognize his voice eventually, but he wasn't going to make it easy for her, and he didn't want recognition to come too soon.

That would spoil the fun and he intended to enjoy every stage of Harley's undoing.

"I don't want you to be scared." He traced a path back and forth across the soft skin above her knee with his thumb. "Is there anything I can do to put your mind at ease?"

Her tongue slipped out.

The sight of her pink tongue caressing her full lips was sexy as hell, a fact he was certain she was aware of, no matter how unpracticed the movement seemed.

"I d-don't know." She took a deep breath, her full breasts rising and falling.

He glanced down at the tempting cleavage visible above the tight bodice of her dress and tried not to think about how much he wanted her gorgeous tits heavy in his hands.

"I um…" She swallowed. "I've n-never done anything like this before."

"I know." He allowed his thumb to slide higher on her bare thigh.

Her legs remained close together, not tightening to bar his passage, but not parting to invite him in, the perfect balance of coy and seductive, proving Harley was still at the top of her game.

"But you did very well in the hotel room," he added.

"I was scared to death," she whispered.

"I couldn't tell," he lied. "I thought you were beautiful and very, very sexy."

She took a breath, holding it for a moment before she said in a husky voice, "It would help if I could see your face."

"Not yet," he said. "Soon, but first I want you to help me live out a fantasy I've had for a long time."

She tensed again but nodded, slowly. "A-all right."

"I've always wanted to be the stranger on the train," he said, stroking a little higher on her thigh as his other hand reached up to release her seatbelt. "I've always wanted to make a woman come before we've even kissed. Before she's so much as seen my face."

"That's the reason for the blindfold," she said, her shoulders relaxing slightly, seemingly comforted by the confession.

"That's the reason for the blindfold," he lied again. "And why I'm going to ask you to spread your legs for me."

"Now?" Her throat worked.

"Now," he said. "There aren't any midnight trains on the Tahitian islands, so we're going to have to settle for a private plane. Now spread your legs, Hannah, show me that beautiful pussy."

Harley's fingers tightened on the arms of her chair and her jaw locked.

Even with her eyes covered, he could tell her expression was that of someone who'd taken a bite of something rotten and was too mannerly to spit it out.

He expected her to deny him, to force him to ask again—maybe even threaten to take the money back if she didn't obey—but after a moment she slowly spread her legs, parting her thighs for him, granting him his first glimpse of her pussy.

But a glimpse wasn't enough.

"Wider," he whispered, exerting the slightest pressure on the knee he cupped in his hand. "And move to the edge of the seat."

With a shaky breath, she obeyed, shifting her hips and spreading her legs wide enough for her skirt to bunch up around her waist, revealing her pink outer lips and the entrance to the pussy that had haunted his dreams.

She was fucking beautiful, delicate and deadly, like a flower infused with poison.

Hers was a pussy men would kill for, one he might have died for if she'd decided to frame him for murder instead of rape.

Her lips were fuller than he remembered

and her sex was quiet and shuttered against him, but soon he'd have her swollen and wet.

Soon he'd have her panting and begging for him to bring her over.

And then he would.

Again and again.

Until his hand was sticky with her desire.

He wanted her thighs dripping and her body hungry for more when he removed the blindfold.

He wanted her to know she'd already lost the first battle the moment he declared war.

CHAPTER NINE

Jackson

"Lovely," he murmured.

He worked his hands up the insides of her thighs, kneading her muscled flesh as he drew closer to her apex, his cock thickening from a potent combination of lust and this first heady taste of revenge. "You have a beautiful body."

"Thank you," she whispered in a strained voice, her fingers curling tighter around her armrests.

She looked like she was bracing herself for a beating.

"Relax, beautiful, I know what I'm doing. This is going to feel good."

She nodded slightly. "O-okay…"

"But?" He hesitated, urging her legs still

wider, but not moving his fingers to her delicate flesh.

"I wish I could see you," she said softly. "Just your eyes, just for a second."

"And why's that?" He traced a fingertip down the seam of her thigh, inches from where her leg became something more intimate.

She tensed but didn't try to close her thighs. "You can read so much about someone from their eyes, don't you think?"

"Not as much as you can read from a touch," he said, bringing his thumb to her clit and circling gently, making her gulp for her next breath. "Don't worry about my eyes. Concentrate on my touch. Let me bring you pleasure."

She didn't respond.

But she didn't need to, her body assured him she was obeying his command.

Slowly, but surely, she blossomed beneath his touch.

Her clit hardened against his thumb, her sex flushed a deeper pink, and within minutes telltale slickness glistened at the entrance to her cunt.

Jackson wanted to bend down and lick her wetness away, to burrow his tongue into her pussy so deep he would be able to feel her muscles contract when she came, but oral sex was too intimate.

Oral sex was an offering, a humbling of yourself in the name of pleasuring your lover.

Harley would take his cock down her throat when he was ready, but he wouldn't put his mouth on her while they were together.

She would get his hands or his cock.

He didn't intend to kiss her on the lips, let alone anywhere else.

Kisses were for people you trusted and cared for. Harley was neither and any pleasure he gave her would be in the name of breaking her down.

Her desire would be his weapon and her orgasms instruments of her own destruction.

"I love seeing you wet," he said. "But I want you even wetter."

He brought his free hand to her entrance, teasing the edges of her slick cleft before sliding one finger into her heat, all the way up to the knuckle.

She gasped and her head fell back as he fucked her with his hand, all while maintaining his patient torture of her clit, applying enough pressure to drive her higher, but not enough to take her over the edge.

He added a second finger, looked up to see her breasts rising and falling faster, and suddenly couldn't tolerate that part of her being hidden from his gaze.

He grasped the top of her dress and pulled it down with a sharp tug. Her heavy breasts fell free, bobbing gently as she cried out.

She moved instinctively to cover herself, but he captured her wrist in a firm grip.

"Hands at your sides," he ordered, his voice thick and his pulse speeding as she obeyed him.

Yes, this is what he needed.

He needed her tits in his hands, her wetness coating his fingers.

But most of all he needed her submission.

He needed her stripped bare and vulnerable by the time they landed and the flight wasn't a long one.

"These are mine and I'll touch them when I choose." He shifted his angle of penetration, bringing his left thumb to her clit as his left fingers continued to drive in and out of her pussy, leaving his right hand free to play.

He cupped her breast in his hand, capturing her already puckered nipple between his fingertips. He pinched her flesh hard enough to make her gasp, then pinched it even harder before rolling the bud in a fierce circle between his finger and thumb.

He was rewarded with a moan wrenched

from the back of Harley's throat and a rush of heat between her legs.

"Your tits are mine and your cunt is mine," he said, slipping a third finger into her pussy.

He could feel her desire-plumped flesh stretching to accommodate the thickness between her legs.

"For the next month, you will belong to me," he continued. "Your body will be my playground and your pleasure my property. You will not touch yourself while you're with me and you will come only when you're allowed to come. Do you understand me, Hannah?"

"Yes," she said, her hips lifting into his thrusts.

"Yes, sir," he corrected, transferring his attention to her other breast, plucking at her erect nipple. "You will show me respect, especially in the bedroom."

"Yes, sir," she said, lips parting as her breath came faster. "Yes, sir, please, sir."

"Please what?" he asked.

His cock was so hard it throbbed painfully, aching to be buried in the pussy gushing slick honey onto his hand.

"Please, I-I can't stop," she panted. "I'm going to come."

"No, you're not. Wait until I give you

permission," he commanded even as he picked up his pace, fucking her hard and deep with his fingers. "Wait or you'll be punished."

"Yes, sir," she said, features twisting as she spread her legs even wider, welcoming his rough use. "Oh God, sir. Please. Oh my God!"

Jackson's lips twisted.

He *was* her God.

And soon she'd be prostrate on the ground before him, begging him for mercy.

The irony was so perfect he decided to let her off easy.

There would be time to delay her pleasure and drag out her suffering later.

Now, he wanted to watch her come and know he was only minutes away from the revelations that would leave her trembling with terror and ashamed of how easily she'd become his whore.

"Come, Hannah," her owner ordered in that insanely sexy voice of his, the one that was familiar and foreign, arousing and terrifying, all at the same time. "Come hard for me."

She obeyed with a rough cry, her pussy locking down around his fingers, coating him in her juices. She was so wet it would be embarrassing if she had any room left in her mind for worry or shame.

But there was only pleasure, white hot and electric, and bliss overloading her nervous system until she felt she might die from it.

She squirmed and moaned beneath his fingers as he continued to drive in and out of her heated flesh.

She spun through a dizzy world of pleasure

for what felt like hours—her womb pulsing and her nipples burning beneath his wicked, teasing fingers. But she still hadn't made it all the way back to earth when he moved his hand from her breast to her clit, pinching the erect nub between his fingers, dragging her back into the overwhelming spin of bliss.

This time, she reached for him as her pleasure claimed her. Her fingers found his upper arms and dug into the muscles there, not surprised to find he was as huge as she'd guessed. His biceps were rock hard, without a pinch of fat to soften his flesh.

Based on the feel of those arms alone, he was easily twice her size. Twice her size and terrifyingly strong, but she couldn't bring herself to be afraid.

Logically she knew she should be wary that he had claimed her body and pleasure as his property and demanded her compliance without any assurances to keep her safe while she was in his keeping. But something inside her insisted that any man who could bring her such exquisite pleasure wasn't someone she should fear.

And something else inside her—that veiled part only one man had ever tapped into on that stolen night long ago—reveled in being controlled.

In her deepest, most private fantasies, she didn't dream of candlelit dinners and gentle kisses.

She dreamed of strong hands, a commanding voice, and a lover who would demand her submission and reward her obedience.

Maybe that's why it hadn't been as hard to put herself up for sale as it should have been.

She was a self-respecting woman. She didn't want to be a man's whore, but in her secret heart, she did yearn to be owned.

And now she was, by a man who gently set her hands back on her armrests before pulling her clothes back into place—top of her dress tugged up and her skirt eased down over her still trembling thighs just as the air pressure in the cabin began to shift.

"We're nearly there," he said as he buckled her seatbelt across her waist once more. "Are you ready for a surprise?"

"What kind of surprise, sir?" she asked softly, suddenly shy. It was so strange, to have been pleasured by a man who she knew only by touch and sound.

It made her feel exposed and off-center, but at the same time strangely powerful.

She could tell that she'd pleased him.

She'd heard it in his grunt of approval

when she'd so eagerly called him "sir," and in the rich timbre of his voice when he'd ordered her to come. It gave her hope that maybe this month wouldn't pass as miserably as she'd expected.

Maybe she and this man would find their sexual appetites compatible.

Maybe they would even become...friends.

Odd, unexpected friends, but friends nevertheless.

The hope made her heart lighter, but it also made her vulnerable.

She was unprepared for the sudden shift in her mystery man's tone, her thoughts too muddled by pleasure to make sense of his words when he said—

"An unpleasant surprise. At least for you."

She frowned beneath her blindfold, her pulse picking up again. "Why? Didn't I please you, sir?"

"You pleased me very much. Today." He spoke louder to be heard over the dull roar of the landing gear descending from beneath the plane, sounding less gruff than he had before.

"But this isn't about today, beautiful," he continued. "It's about penance for the sins of the past."

A sour taste filled her mouth as she cursed herself for being so ridiculously naïve.

She was here to play her part in fantasies this man had been willing to pay a *million* dollars for her to help him fulfill. She'd been a fool to think this was about anything so relatively tame as Dominance and submission.

But still, she had to hold onto hope that she could find a way to please him, to mollify him, to do whatever it took to ensure she returned to her safe place in the world with her mind and body intact.

"What do you mean, sir?" she asked, clutching her armrests tighter as the plane dipped toward the ground. "What sins?"

"Do you really need me to tell you?" he asked, his voice closer than it had been before, making her think he was leaning across the small space that separated their seats. "Can't you think of a thing or two you should atone for, sweetheart? Haven't you done something in your twenty-eight years of life on this earth that you regret?"

She swallowed. "I've done lots of things I regret. But I've never intentionally hurt someone and I've apologized for my mistakes whenever I could. In my mind, a person can't do much more than that when it comes to atonement, sir."

He chuckled softly, but she couldn't tell if he was amused or angry.

For the hundredth time, she wished she could see his face. Just for a moment. But she knew better than to reach for her blindfold before he'd given her the order.

Her owner had proven he could give her great pleasure, but she sensed he wouldn't hesitate to deliver punishment, as well.

"You really have no shame, do you?" he asked, but before she could answer the wheels connected with the ground and the roar of the plane's brakes fighting their forward momentum made speech impossible.

Eventually, the plane slowed and the pilot's voice came over the intercom. "The car is already waiting, sir. Would you like me to have Jean Pierre meet us at the end of the runway, or do you have business you need to conclude?"

"If you're asking if we're fucking, the answer is no, Adam," her owner said, his irritation clear. "Have JP bring the car around. I'm ready to get Miss North settled in her new home."

Hannah brought her hands to her lap, unbuckling her belt then fighting the urge to fidget with the straps.

She sensed she should keep her mouth shut, but she couldn't help asking, "Is it okay for me to take the blindfold off now, sir?"

"Not yet," he said briskly. "But soon. The house is only a fifteen-minute drive from the airstrip. I want us to be alone when you see my face. I don't want to share that moment with anyone, beautiful. That's just for you and me."

Hannah nodded and tried to smile, but her lips refused to cooperate.

His words were kind enough, but there was something in his tone that brought all her misgivings rising to the surface again.

What if he was hideously disfigured and intended to punish her for all the women who had refused to look beneath his superficial ugliness?

What if he had a grudge against the female sex in general and planned to take his grievances out on the whore he'd bought for the month?

Then you'll show him that you're different.

You'll prove to him that you're grateful for his kindness and the pleasure he gives you.

You'll make him see you as a person with integrity who doesn't deserve to pay penance for the people who have hurt him.

She heard the door to the plane open and a moment later smelled sea air, damp earth, and lush vegetation. But aside from the soft voices of two men conferring outside the door and the distant screeches and warbles of birds, there wasn't another sound to be heard.

The fact that she was on a private island hit home in a new way, making her shiver despite the steamy humidity creeping in to muddy the plane's conditioned air.

She was going to be completely alone here with this man, surrounded by people paid to do his bidding.

Adam had made it clear he honored his employer's wishes without question and she had no doubt the other people in his employ would be the same. Mr. X didn't seem like the type of man who brooked opposition from anyone, let alone the people who worked for him.

She would find no allies among the residents of this island, no one to aid her if she reached out a hand, no one who would care if she cried out for help.

Her fate was truly in the hands of the man who gently, but firmly, took her elbow, helping her rise from her chair before leading her toward the door.

"Bend your head a bit," he said. "Now take the first step down with your left foot. There are four steps down to the ground."

She minded quickly, without question, which was a good thing considering Mr. X didn't slow his pace or make any other concessions for her lack of sight aside from the hand on her arm.

Thanks to her swift obedience she made it safely out of the plane, across the pavement, and into the expensive smelling car waiting for them not far away without tripping or falling flat on her face.

As her owner settled beside her and the car pulled away down a gravel road, she prayed that her obedience would be enough to keep her safe as she started this month-long odyssey with a man who owned her—body and soul.

CHAPTER ELEVEN

Jackson

He had planned to remove the blindfold on the plane, but that was before Harley made the mistake of pretending to be a decent human being. Before she professed in that sweet and sexy voice of hers that she'd never intentionally hurt another person and always apologized for her mistakes.

As if an apology would have been enough to right the wrongs she'd perpetrated against him, even if she'd offered it.

Which she hadn't.

She had ruined his life, potentially killed his best friend—he didn't know if the wreck had been part of the plan or if Clay was just another casualty in Harley's quest for Jackson's destruction—and walked away without a backward glance. And now she was going to pay for it. Her game was over. It was time for his game to begin and he was going to be sure she realized that in a very visceral way.

As soon as they pulled up at the house, he practically dragged her out of the car and up the wide wooden steps leading to the spacious front lanai, where succulent tropical plants in massive planters lent stateliness to the entryway. He pushed through the heavy wooden front door and hurried toward the master bedroom without taking time to appreciate that the home was even more stunning in person than it had been in pictures.

He didn't pause to admire the beautiful central room with the atrium that let in natural light, the gently whirring bamboo fans, or the peaceful indoor pool at the center of the space. He didn't stop to greet the small, aging housekeeper with the steel streaked bun who stood silently in one corner of the expansive kitchen as he charged through, tugging a blindfolded woman behind him.

The housekeeper had known what she was getting into when she took this job. All of the staff had. They'd worked for a South American drug lord, before Jackson, and a contract killer who specialized in discreet murders for the very wealthy before that. They knew the rules.

They would perform their duties, avert their eyes, and stay out of his business, and in exchange they would be paid handsomely and live to service another monster for double the salary of their straight-shooting counterparts. He could kill Harley and bury her body in the jungle behind the mansion and the men and women he'd brought with him to the private island wouldn't lift a hand to stop him.

The thought made his hand tighten around Harley's as he strode down a wide hallway with dark wooden walls to the master suite at the end. She deserved to die for what she'd done, but that wasn't in his game plan.

Death was too good for her. Too peaceful. He was going to break her down, force her to acknowledge the darkness inside of her, and then feed her soul, piece by piece, through the shredder, until she was too shattered to face her reflection in the mirror. He wanted every waking moment of her life to be a punishment to be endured, not a gift to be enjoyed.

He would make her suffer, make her sorry, make her wish she'd never been born. But most importantly, he would make her repent for what she'd done to him or drive them both out of their minds trying.

As soon as he reached the bedroom, he stepped through the door and closed it firmly behind him before recapturing Harley's hand and leading her deeper into the space. When they reached the center of the generous suite, near two small couches and a glass coffee table arranged in front of floor to ceiling windows that showcased a breathtaking view of the lush back lawn, he released Harley's hand.

With his fingers digging firmly into her shoulders, he turned her to face him, his breath coming faster and his heart thudding heavily in his chest.

"Is everything okay, sir?" she asked, in that soft, submissive voice of hers, the one that was innocence and sex mixed into a potent cocktail that had kept his dick hard for most of the past hour.

Even with her eyes covered, she had read him like an open book and adapted to meet his unique needs in less time than it took most people to eat a meal. She clearly had a gift for giving men what they wanted, but it was all an act. Her perfection was only skin deep. In truth, she was a chimera, a mirage, a beautiful illusion that would linger just out of reach until the day she drew her weapon and plunged it into your heart.

"Sir?" she asked again, her arms beginning to tremble at her sides.

"Quiet," he said, his voice hoarse and his breath still labored. He bench pressed well over two-hundred pounds and ran ten miles every day, rarely breaking a sweat until mile three, but his training hadn't prepared him for Harley.

This was more than a battle of bodies. It was a battle of wills, of souls, and it was time she realized that hers belonged to him. She wouldn't set the tone of their relationship. She wouldn't be the puppeteer pulling the strings. She was his property and she would show him her true colors or he'd beat them out of her.

"Stop pretending," he said. "Stop trying to manipulate me. That isn't going to happen this time, sweetheart."

Her breath sped, her chest rising and falling faster, but her trembling ceased. "I don't understand, sir."

"That's because you're a dumb cunt," he said, enjoying her flinch in response to his hard words. "Now drop the act and show me the vindictive, psychotic bitch I bought. She's the one I want right now."

She shook her head ever so slightly and a sob escaped her parted lips. "I don't understand."

"You said that already," he snapped. "Stop playing dumb and don't you dare cry or I'll give you something to cry about."

Her bottom lip quivered as she shook her head again. "I'm not playing, I swear! I just want to please you. I want to make you happy so you won't hurt me. Please." She paused, lips pressing together and her throat working as she fought to keep her tears at bay. "Please, sir. Please, believe me."

"Believe you." He laughed softly, an ugly laugh ripe with his barely suppressed rage. He reached out, driving his fingers into her hair and fisting his hand at the nape of her neck, drawing a mewl of surprise from her full lips.

"I will never believe you," he said, pressing his cheek tightly to hers and whispering his words into her ear. "You will never have power over me and the sooner you realize that, the better. Now, you will show me the woman I want to see, show me the monster beneath your pretty face, or you will suffer the consequences."

She whimpered. "Who do you want to see? Who do you want me to be?"

"Yourself!" he shouted, triggering a full-body cringe from the treacherous woman in his arms. "Be yourself! Stop denying who you are!"

"I am myself!" she shouted back, heat creeping into her tone. "I can't be something I'm not. I'm not the woman who hurt you. I'm Hannah. I'm a good person. I swear I—"

With a growl of rage, Jackson tightened his grip in her hair and jerked down, forcing her to her knees in front of him. She landed with a cry he barely heard over the blood rushing in his ears.

"You are not a good person," he seethed. "I know who you are and I will hear your true name from your own lips. Right now."

She went very still and he could practically hear the wheels turning in her clever head. "Who are you? Why have you brought me here?"

"Right now I want to hear you say your name," he said, ignoring her first question, knowing the truth would be revealed soon enough. "You will not think beyond what I demand of you in any given moment. Your will is mine. Now give me what I want or you will be punished."

With a deep breath, she lifted her chin, somehow managing to project defiance even while on her knees. "Then punish me. I'm not going to play this insane game. I'm not going to pretend to be anyone but who I am. I am

Hannah North, and I don't deserve to be treated this way."

"Punishment it is then," he said, reaching for his belt buckle. "Take your dress off. Now," he added when she hesitated a beat too long. "You chose punishment, Hannah, and I'll have you naked to take it. Unless you're ready to give me what I want."

Her lips tight and her stubborn jaw set, she reached for the top of her dress and tugged it down her curves until it fell around her knees then reached down to guide it back down her calves. Jackson watched her bare her heart-stopping curves as he opened his fly and shoved his pants and boxers around his hips, freeing his aching length.

His cock bobbed free, the swollen flesh pulsing and eager. His dick didn't care that he hated this woman. It was desperate to be buried between her legs, shoving into her hot mouth, sliding between her oil-slicked tits, whatever would get him off the fastest. But this wasn't about pleasure—though he fully intended to come—and he had to maintain control, to prove to both Harley and himself that he was in charge.

"Touch your nipples," he said, bringing one hand to his cock and beginning to stroke his own engorged length. "Pinch them, make them tight for me."

Harley slowly brought her hands to her breasts but when her fingers captured her nipples it was clear her heart wasn't in it. She only lightly stroked the pink flesh and her skin remained flat and unresponsive.

"Harder," he said. "I want your pussy wet the way it was on the plane. I want you dripping down your thighs and your cunt hungry for something to fill it."

"I don't want to have sex with you," she said, voice trembling. "Not like this."

"We're not going to have sex," he said, kneeling in front of her. "When I finally fuck you, you will have been begging for it for days. You will be so desperate for my cock, you'll lick the bathroom floor clean if that's what it takes to get me to put it in you."

Her lips puckered, but she didn't speak a word. She didn't have to.

"You think I'm lying," he said, stroking his cock a little faster, aroused by the thought of her begging. "But I'm not. I will not take you by force. I won't have to. Now pinch your nipples for me. That's right. Like that. Now harder."

She obeyed and slowly a telltale flush spread across her chest and her breath came faster. He waited until she was biting her bottom lip and her thighs were clenching and releasing, causing her hips to shift slightly, before issuing his next order.

"Lie back and spread your legs." She hesitated, but he pushed on before she could protest. "Right now, Hannah, or I may rethink my promise not to fuck you on the floor."

Her flush spreading up her neck, she lay back on the floor and spread her legs barely two hand widths apart, playing the prude though it was clear she was turned on.

"Wider, Hannah," he said. "Grab the back of your knees and pull toward your shoulders. I want to see every inch of my pussy."

She moved slowly, efficiently, clearly doing her best not to put on a show for him, but seeing her spread wide, revealing her most intimate places made his cock leap in his hand.

Fuck, she was even hotter than she used to be, so curvy and plush and obedient. He took a deep breath, forcing himself to slow his rhythm, to ease his grip on his swollen shaft. He was going to have his release, but first, he needed her to beg him for it.

And he knew exactly how to make her beg. Harley had played him for the worst sort of fool, but the passion between them had always been real. She hated him, but that hadn't cooled her lust any more than it cooled his own.

And now he was going to use his intimate knowledge of how his kinky little bitch liked it to begin bringing her under his thumb.

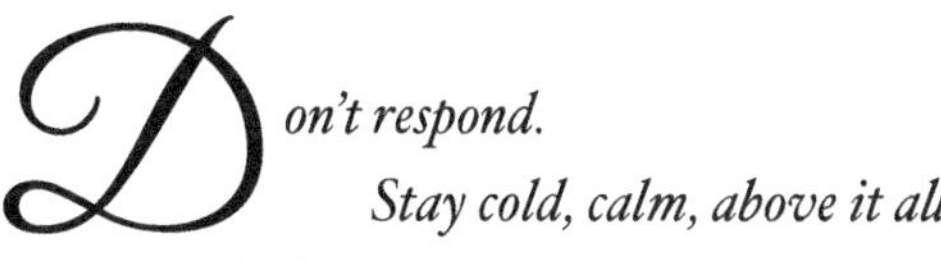

Don't respond.

Stay cold, calm, above it all.

Don't let him get to you.

Hannah squeezed her eyes closed and clenched her jaw, struggling to stay motionless and unaffected as the insane person who'd bought her explored her sex with his long, thick fingers, playing through her folds, dipping into her slickness before circling her clit with a not-quite-firm-enough pressure.

She fought to shut down her nerve endings, but it was no use.

This man was out of his damned mind, cruel, and probably dangerous, but he also knew how to play her like an instrument. He was a maestro and she was helpless to resist the erotic song he coaxed from her body.

Soon, her pussy was dripping and her sex plump and swollen beneath his touch.

She stayed still as long as she could, but eventually she lost the battle against her own desire and lifted her hips, fighting to get closer to the fingers that stroked her clit hard enough to make her crazy, but not firmly enough to grant her relief.

"You want more?" he asked. "More here?" He tapped her clit, making her breath catch. "Tell me, Hannah. Tell me what you want or you won't get it."

"Yes, more," she said, the words transforming to a yelp of pleasure-pain as he smacked her between the legs.

Pain flashed through her sensitive clit to spread through her belly, but it was followed by a rush of even more intense pleasure as his fingers returned to her clit and what felt like his thumb plunged into her pussy.

"Yes, sir," he corrected as he worked her harder, building the need swelling inside her. "Or I'll slap you again. Do you understand, Hannah?"

Hannah bit her lip, fighting the desire washing through her like a hot, sticky flood, a wild thing that didn't care if this man was crazy or dangerous.

That part of her didn't give a shit that this was degrading.

It just wanted him to slap her again.

"Or do you want more punishment?" he asked, proving she was hopelessly easy to read, even with a blindfold covering half her face. "You want more of this?"

He slapped her again, twice in rapid succession and she cried out, but it wasn't a cry of pain. There was no mistaking the lust in the sound.

She sounded like she was about to come and it suddenly wasn't that much of a stretch to imagine herself at his feet begging him to fuck her.

If he teased her like this for too long, she would be so desperate for relief she had no idea what she would do.

"You like me to hurt you a little don't you?" he asked, his breath coming faster, making her think he was turned on, too.

As messed up as he was, he seemed to get off on her pleasure, not her fear, which she could only hope meant he didn't intend to rape her.

It wouldn't be rape.

If he pushed his cock inside you right now, you wouldn't fight.

You'd beg him not to stop.

The thought made tears rise in her eyes and her face feel lava hot.

What the hell was wrong with her?

How could she be falling so easily under this man's twisted spell?

"Answer me, when I speak to you," he demanded, swatting her two, three, four times between the legs, until her clit burned and the delicate skin around her pussy grew hot from the repeated contact.

"Yes, sir," she panted, squirming her hips though she wasn't sure if she was trying to get closer or farther away.

The sensations he aroused in her were dizzying, making her feel outside herself and more in touch with her own desire all at the same time.

"Yes," she sad. "I like it when you slap me."

"What about when I slap you here?"

Hannah cried out again as his big hand slapped first her right breast and then her left, rippling her flesh and making her nipples pull so tight they ached.

Ached for more.

Ached for that heady sting and then his mouth hot on her puckered skin, taking the pain away.

"Yes, sir. Please, sir," she said, her hunger peaking as his fingers set a faster pace between her legs, fucking her hard, but not hard enough.

Shamelessly, she spread her legs wider, silently begging for what she wanted, but she should have known her tormentor wouldn't be satisfied with silence.

"Please, what?" he asked. "You want to come?"

"Yes, please. Please, sir!"

"You've already come twice in the plane," he said, his voice husky with the same desire that was driving her crazy. "I think it's my turn, first, don't you?"

"Yes," she said, reaching for him. "Tell me what you want me to do."

"I want you to put your hands back on your nipples," he said. "Then I want you to beg me to come on your tits."

She moved her hands, but when she opened her mouth the words wouldn't come.

She'd never said the word "tits" before in her entire life and she'd never been overly verbal in bed. Sighs, moans, and the occasional, "yes, there, more please," were the extent of her dirty talk.

She was still trying to get her mouth to form the uncomfortable phrase when her tormentor suddenly pulled his hand away from her pussy, leaving her feeling bereft and abandoned.

And so damned unsatisfied, she couldn't stifle the groan of protest that escaped her lips.

"If you want to come, you need to beg," he said, his voice underscored by the faint sound of flesh sliding against flesh, making her think he was touching himself somewhere nearby.

The thought was unexpectedly, intensely arousing.

She wondered what he looked like, kneeling over her prone body, his cock in his hand, stroking himself while he watched her roll her nipples between her fingertips.

Imagining it made her even hotter and her wild, primitive side ached to drop her hands between her legs and bring herself over at the same moment he did.

But that wasn't what he wanted.

He wanted her to beg and suddenly she wanted it too. She wanted whatever it was he needed to get off, to lose some of that fierce control and come because she had *made* him come.

"Come on my tits, sir," she said, her voice breathy and strained as she rolled her nipples in firmer circles. "Please come on my tits. Please. I want to feel you."

The sounds of flesh against flesh grew more urgent and when he spoke his sexy voice was an even sexier growl. "More. Beg me, Hannah. Make me feel how much you want me to cover you with my cum."

"Please, sir," she begged, her thighs clenching and releasing as the tension building inside of her became almost unbearable. "Please come on my tits. Cover me, mark me. I want you hot on my skin, I want to feel your—"

He cut her off with a groan and a second later she felt his hot stickiness splash across her chest, covering her hands and her breasts in his release, making her gasp and her clit throb.

He smelled like fresh cut grass and lemons and something fiercely, unrepentantly male and his labored breath was music to her ears.

If you'd asked her beforehand, she would have assumed having a stranger come on her chest would be distasteful at best and revolting at worst.

But right now all she felt was turned on. She could come from a single finger pressed against her clit, but only *his* finger.

She needed him to touch her, to bring her over until she was panting on the floor beside him.

Her nerve endings buzzed and hummed with longing and her sex was so swollen and heavy her longing was quickly approaching suffering. It felt like there was a burning stone weighing down her pelvis and he was the only one who could take the pain away and replace it with pleasure.

"Can I come now, sir?" she asked, teeth digging into her bottom lip as her thighs clenched together, seeking relief. "Please, sir?"

"In a moment," he said. "But first, I want you to see my face. Are you ready, Hannah?"

"Yes." Her tongue slipped out to dampen her lips and her pulse fluttered in her neck.

She was nervous, but she was also excited, ready to see the face of this man who both enraged and seduced her so easily.

And scared her, she shouldn't forget about that, but with the magic he'd set loose in her body making her high with desire, it was hard to remember to be afraid.

How could she fear a man who, thus far, had given her the greatest pleasure she'd ever experienced?

Bar one night, one man, and she knew by now that no one would ever live up to him, to that intense sexual encounter so long ago that never should have happened in the first place.

She was thinking of him as her owner untied her blindfold.

She was thinking of his incomparable body and sharply angled face.

Of those eyes that were both hungry and devoted, predatory and so full of love she would have sold her soul to exchange places with her sister, to be the Mason twin that beautiful stranger loved with such devotion and intensity.

She was so lost in the memory that for a moment, when her blurred vision cleared and she looked up into the face of her captor, she was certain she was hallucinating.

It couldn't be...

There was no possible way...

Her eyes widened and her heart raced, slamming against her ribs, excitement and confusion making her feel like she was being pulled in two.

It couldn't be him, but still...there he was, standing over her, zipping up his gray suit pants and pulling his belt back into place.

His eyes were harder, his face covered in dark stubble, and his body even thicker and more powerful than she remembered beneath his button down shirt, but he was her stranger, there was no doubt about it.

He had come for her, bought her, and taken her away.

And now he wanted to punish her for her sins.

He must know that it hadn't been Harley he was with that last night. He must know it and be sufficiently enraged by it that he had tracked her down and done whatever it took to get her isolated on this island and at his mercy.

Hiro must have been complicit in the scheme, which meant Aunt Sybil might not be safe.

Hannah knew she should be worried about Sybil, concerned for her own safety, and terrified of this man who was clearly as obsessive and mad as he was gorgeous. But she had been waiting years to see his face again, to feel his hands on her, his body moving inside of her, his rough voice calling her name instead of her sister's.

And the part of her that had meant her promise to belong to him forever didn't feel afraid.

She felt like she was coming home, finding something precious she'd thought was lost forever.

So when she met his gaze and saw the

hard, challenging expression in his eyes, her stomach flipped with excitement, not terror.

She would be his for an entire month and she would finally learn his name.

It wasn't much.

But for a woman who had dreamed only of *his* hands since the night he crawled out that window into the rain, it was a gift.

A dark gift, but a gift nevertheless.

And when a person receives a gift, there's nothing to do but smile.

CHAPTER THIRTEEN

Jackson

*J*ackson waited, watching Harley's eyes widening in recognition, not wanting to miss the moment she realized she had been caught in an inescapable snare.

Her hair was wild around her face and her eyes glittered in the sunset light streaming through the windows, making her look like a goddess come down to earth. Even sprawled on the floor, covered in cum, and with lines on her forehead where the blindfold was tied too tightly she was beautiful.

Those signs of his use made her even more beautiful, and if she were one of the submissive lovers he'd enjoyed himself with during his travels, he would be proud of her for her obedience and the way she'd relished the feel of him marking her with his release.

But she wasn't his lover, she was his enemy and any moment her nimble mind would work its way around to the truth and she would shatter before him. She would quake and beg and know with a bone-deep certainty that all her worst nightmares had come true.

He expected her cheeks to pale and her lips to tremble. At the very least, he expected denial and pointless explanations. He didn't expect her to smile.

But she did.

She smiled.

She smiled like the sun coming out from behind a rain cloud, a relieved, helpless-to-stop-its-spread, hopeful smile that left him feeling like he'd been punched in the gut.

The bitch actually looked happy to see him. Legitimately happy.

Not vindictively happy, not wickedly happy, just pleased.

Grateful even.

What the fuck.

What. The unholy. Fuck.

Jackson and Hannah's story continues in

DEEP DOMINATION
Available now.

Keep reading for a Sneak Peek of
Deep Domination, book two in the
Bought by the Billionaire series.

WARNING: This is one deep, dark, hard-spanking, dirty-talking read. Are you ready?

Hannah is in too deep, falling steadily under Jackson's erotic control.

It doesn't matter that he's her captor and tormentor. She lives for the nights when he draws her deeper into his world, teaching her the thrill of submission

Pain and pleasure.

Love and hate.

Him and her.

Jackson is falling—remembering why he couldn't get enough of the woman who destroyed him—but so is she.

Soon, he'll reach Hannah's hard limit and her obedient façade will fall away, exposing the monster he's hunted across three continents.

But soon a shocking revelation interrupts their dark and twisted game and Jackson is left wondering who is the true monster.

Hannah

Her stranger was clearly angry—furious—but Hannah couldn't have stopped the smile blossoming across her face if she'd tried.

It was really him, *him*, the man she'd tried to convince herself she wasn't obsessed with for six long years.

The stranger who had laid claim to her body, captured her imagination, and haunted her dreams.

No...he had haunted her awakenings.

In her dreams, one glimpse of his face and she was electrified by pleasure. In dreams she was transported to the heaven of his arms, blessed by belonging to him in a way she'd never belonged to anyone, not even herself.

It was waking up and realizing that the one night they'd shared had been a lie and that she would never see him again that was hell.

She'd always known that night was a lie, but now maybe he knew it too.

Maybe *that's* why he'd come for her.

Her smile vanished so quickly it sent a flash of discomfort through her cheeks.

Hannah stared up at him, watching his jaw clench and storm clouds roll in behind his dark eyes. She cringed, wishing she could melt through the floor or that she at least had a blanket to pull across her body to shield her nakedness.

But the polished hardwood held firm beneath her back and she remained exposed to her stranger, his release cooling on her bare chest as he glared down at her, his hands tightening into fists.

She half expected him to strike her, to drive his fist into her stomach as punishment for the smile she hadn't been able to control.

Instead, he squatted on his heels beside her, moving with a slow, easy grace that sent a chill across her flesh. She felt hunted, but there was nowhere to run.

He owned her.

He had bought and paid for the privilege of enacting his revenge and now her life was in his hands.

He would decide whether the next month would pass in pleasure or pain.

He would decide how she would pay for her sins and whether she would leave this island alive.

The thought of him beating the life out of her with his large hands made her whimper, even before he brought one of them to her throat.

His grip was loose, but his fingers were so long they completely encircled her neck, bringing her claustrophobia surging back with a vengeance, making her blood race and her head spin as he leaned down to whisper inches from her face.

"I will tell you this one time and one time only, so listen closely," he said, his voice thick with rage, but so smooth and controlled it somehow made his next words even more frightening. "I am not the man I was before. There is no softness in my heart for you. There is no heart left to soften. I am beyond your reach. I own you and I intend to break you and nothing you do will change your fate. Do you understand?"

Hannah nodded as she swallowed convulsively, fighting to keep her breath under control as anxiety electrified her nerve endings.

"You can smile while I break you or you can cry," he continued, a smile curving his lips. "But the ending will be the same."

His grip tightened, not enough to hurt, but enough to make Hannah's anxiety creep toward full-blown panic.

She was seconds from clawing at his fingers, when he suddenly released her and stood, wiping his hands on his neatly pressed pants, as if touching her had dirtied them in some way.

"Clean up. The bathroom should have everything you need," he said, pointing toward the opposite side of the room. "After you shower, you will stay in this room until granted permission to leave."

He turned to go, but stopped before he'd taken five steps and spun back to face her, making Hannah's slowing pulse lurch back into high gear. "And if I learn you've disobeyed my order—any order I give you while you're here—all the promises I've made to you will be invalidated. Think about that before you try to run. Because I will find you, Harley, and my punishment will make it clear how gentle I've been with you so far."

Harley?

Hannah's brows drew together, but she didn't say a word.

She didn't know what to say, what to think.

She only knew that she wouldn't be able to organize her thoughts as long as he was in the room. His rage was a fire that sucked all the oxygen from the air and left her gasping, as shocked and confused as a fish dangling from the end of a fisherman's hook.

It wasn't until the heavy door closed behind him and she heard his footsteps moving away down the hall that she dared to drag her trembling body into a seated position.

Her movement set his seed sliding down the front of her chest.

A wave of self-loathing turned her stomach as memories of their brief time together raced through her head.

He must have thought she was Harley from the beginning.

That's why he'd kept insisting that she say her name and been so angry when she maintained that she was Hannah North. She'd thought maybe he was one of her family's enemies and wanted confirmation that she was a Mason, not a North, but he'd been waiting for her to confess that she was her sister.

Somehow, he didn't know that her twin was dead and was clearly committed to punishing Harley for whatever sins she had perpetrated against him.

Hannah would have liked to believe her sister was innocent of whatever had turned her commanding, but once beautifully passionate, stranger into a terrifying man bent on revenge, but she knew better. She would always love her sister and grieve the fact that Harley had been taken away from her too soon, but she didn't believe in revisionist history.

Dying hadn't changed the person her twin had been before she was murdered.

And Harley had been a spiteful, inexorable, often frightening force of nature. She had played with men's hearts like a twisted child who enjoys torturing animals before putting the poor creatures out of their misery.

Their shared psychiatrist had said Harley's rough handling of romantic relationships was her way of protecting herself from becoming the kind of broken woman their mother had become, but that didn't make Harley's treatment any easier for her victims. Hannah had seen more than one strong man shattered after learning the woman he'd fallen in love with was an illusion and the reality was a sociopath who seemed to gain succor from breaking people's hearts.

Harley had always managed to walk away from the wreckage and disappear before her victim's grief could transform to rage.

But now her sister's bad love karma had caught up with Hannah, who had been paid a million dollars to give a man a shot at vengeance.

Hannah couldn't tell her stranger the truth.

If she told him that she was Harley's twin, not the woman who'd hurt him, she would endanger her and Sybil's future.

He wouldn't want her if he learned the truth. Obviously a surrogate wouldn't suffice or he would have taken out his frustration on other women years ago.

He wanted Harley, the "vindictive, psychotic bitch he'd bought" and no one else would do.

"What did you do to him, Harley?" Hannah whispered as she drew her knees in to her chest, shivering despite the evening sun streaming through the floor to ceiling windows behind her, warming the large room.

Sometimes Hannah would swear she could feel her sister's spirit lingering nearby, not ready to leave until they could go out of the world together, the way they'd come into it, but now the air remained quiet, empty.

She was alone, defenseless, and had no choice but to play a dangerous game with a man incapable of compassion.

But maybe Harley didn't deserve compassion.

Maybe she'd done something so horrible, so unforgivable that retribution was the only fitting response.

And maybe Hannah would have no choice but to pay the price for Harley's mistakes.

As she came to her feet and padded silently toward the bathroom, she hoped she would find a way to survive being shattered by the only man who had ever made her dream about what it would be like to belong to someone—body and soul.

Deep Domination is Available Now.

ACKNOWLEDGMENTS

First and foremost, thank you to my readers. Every email has meant so much.

I can't express how deeply grateful I am for the chance to entertain you.

More big thanks to my Street Team, who I am convinced are the sweetest, funniest, kindest group of people around. You inspire me and keep me going and I'm not sure I'd be one third as productive without you.

Big tackle hugs to all!

More thanks to Kara H. for organizational excellence and helping me get the word out.

(No one would have heard of the books without you!)

Thanks to the Facebook groups who have welcomed me in, to the bloggers who have taken a chance on my work, and to everyone who has taken time out of their day to write and post a review.

Deepest thanks,
Everly

I love reading your thoughts about the books and your review matters. Reviews help readers find new-to-them authors to enjoy. So if you could take a moment to leave a review letting me know your favorite part of the story—nothing fancy required, even a sentence or two would be wonderful—I would be deeply grateful.

ALSO BY EVERLY STONE

Bought by the Billionaire

The Series

(HOT novellas, must be read in order)

Dark Domination

Deep Domination

Desperate Domination

Divine Domination

Kidnapped by the Billionaire

The Series

(HOT novellas, must be read in order)

Filthy Wicked Love

Crazy Beautiful Love

One More Shameless Night

Under His Command

The Series

(HOT novellas, must be read in order)

Controlling her Pleasure

Commanding her Trust

Claiming her Heart

The Snowed in Series

Snowbound with the Billionaire

Snowed in with the Boss